Once upon a time there was an old woman who lived in a vinegar bottle. The vinegar bottle stood by itself on the edge of a wide loch.

It was an old farm building, but the villagers called it the 'vinegar bottle' because vinegar used to be made in thick stone bottles with glazed yellow necks.

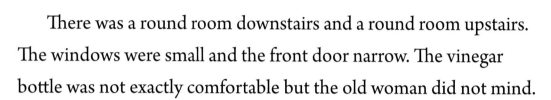

There was a round room downstairs and a round room upstairs.
The windows were small and the front door narrow. The vinegar
bottle was not exactly comfortable but the old woman did not mind.

"There's no place like home," she said.

In the sitting room downstairs were a table and a chair, and she
had made a rag rug to go in front of the fire by her rocking chair.
On the hob, a small black kettle sang to itself all day long and upstairs
on her bed was a patchwork quilt made from pieces of all the dresses
she had owned since she was seven. She had a dustpan and a broom,
and outside hung a tin bathtub.

"What more could anybody want?" asked the old woman.

Though she was poor, the old woman kept the vinegar bottle
specklessly clean, and she spent a good deal of her time picking up
driftwood from the shore or cutting peat. There was no one to help
her because she lived all alone.

"Alone? Not a bit of it. Haven't I got Malt?" said the old woman.

Malt was her cat.

RUMER GODDEN & MAIRI HEDDERWICK

The Old Woman Who Lived in a Vinegar Bottle

The old woman did not have much to eat. Every Monday she went to the village and bought tea, sugar and flour. When she got home she baked two loaves. "They last the week," she said.

When the butchers van came round, she bought leftover meat for Malt. On Tuesdays and Fridays she walked to the farm for milk – most of that went to Malt too. Sometimes the farmer let her collect potatoes left in the field. In autumn she picked blackberries and often found windfall apples in the grass.

"A little more would be good," said the old woman. "But all in all, it's enough for me."

Malt was twice as fat as the old woman.

One Saturday morning, the old woman was hungry. There were only two crusts of bread and a handful of potatoes left. "One for dinner, one for supper. You must make do with that," she told herself and went about her work.

But when the village church clock struck noon she sat down in her rocking chair because she felt a little weak. Malt was curled up on a cushion by the hearth.

It was a fine morning, and the old woman opened the door so she could watch a fishing boat coming in while she rocked: *rock, purr, purr, rock.* Then she stopped.

"Dust!" said the old woman. "Dust on my clean floor!"

She fetched her broom and began to sweep. Suddenly she saw something in the dust, glinting silver in the sun, something small and round.

"Lordy! Well, I never did! A silver sixpence!" she said.

The fishermen had grounded their boat and were unloading
their catch. "I know what I'll do. I'll buy me a fish for my dinner."

As soon as he heard the word 'fish', Malt jumped up and
accompanied the old woman down to the shore.

"Can't buy much of a fish for that," said the fisherman when
the old woman offered the sixpence.

"You can have this little 'un." Another man tossed a small
fish into her hand.

The little fish was still alive, its mouth opening and shutting
while its tail twitched.

"'Tis small for certain," said the old woman. "Still, the middle'll be enough for me, the head and tail for Malt."

She looked at the dying little fish. "I could eat it with tatties..."

But the fish gasped, its tail gave a helpless twitch, and the old woman could not bear it. She ran to the water's edge and threw the little fish, *plop*, back into the loch.

Malt gave a *miaow* of anguish.

The fishermen stared. "Whatever did you do that for?"

Malt stalked away to sulk behind the peat stack.

The old woman was left alone on the shore. She felt old and silly – and hungry. She had just turned to go back to the vinegar bottle when a sound made her stop.

There were ripples in the loch. Then the water went *bubble bubble bubble*, and up came the little fish.

Now it was the old woman who gasped, but the little fish spoke quite calmly.

"Old woman…"

"Yes – sir." She did not know whether to call a fish 'sir' but then she had not known – anywhere in the world – of a fish that could talk.

"You are a dear, kind old woman, and as unselfish as you are kind."

"Thank you … sir."

"You should say 'sire' not 'sir'," said the fish. "Or Highness. I am the ruler of this loch. I look like a fish but I am a prince."

"Lordy!" said the old woman.

"Not a lord, a prince. But no matter," said the fish. "You saved my life, so anything you want, I shall grant."

"Thank you kindly, sir… prince… Highness…" stammered the old woman, "but I don't want anything."

"Well, if you do, come to the shore and call, 'Little fish, little fish,' and I shall come." The fish sank back into the water.

The old woman made a deep curtsey.

Back in the vinegar bottle the old woman sat down in her chair. A fish who was a prince… that talked! "I must have been dreaming," she thought.

But on her hand was the smell of fish and one tiny silver fish scale.

Then her glance fell on Malt's empty cushion. She looked towards the loch, half afraid.

The next minute she was standing on the shore.

"Little fish. Little fish."

The water went *bubble bubble bubble* and up came the fish.

"Excuse me for bothering you … but there is one thing I very
much need." She was twisting her apron into a knot. "You see
there's only two crusts of bread left and hardly any tatties, so…
little fish, sir, Highness, do you think you could give Malt and me
a good hot dinner?"

"Go home and you will find one," said the little fish.

When the old woman arrived home, what a sight met her eyes –
and what a smell! Malt had smelled it too and come running.

There was soup, hot roast beef, roast tatties, greens and gravy.
There was even an apple tart with fresh cream for afters. On the
floor by Malt's cushion was a bowl of meat, a saucer of milk and
a toy mouse.

"Lordy! Lordy! Lordy!" said the old woman.

Malt was already gobbling but, before she touched a morsel,
the old woman went back to the loch and called, "Thank you kindly,"
and curtsied again. After they had eaten, they fell asleep, one each
side of the fire. When they woke up the table was cleared.

A storm blew up on the loch that night and the old woman lay awake listening to the wind and the rain.

"The roof will blow off," she thought. "We shall blow right over."

Malt was not worried; he was sound asleep at the foot of the bed.

Suddenly the old woman sat up. "Lordy! Why didn't I think of that before?"

It was still early when she stood at the water's edge and called, "Little fish, little fish."

The water went *bubble bubble bubble* and up came the little fish.

"If you please, little fish, I'm tired of living in a vinegar bottle. Would it be too much trouble to let me have a little cottage?" pleaded the old woman.

"Go home and you will find one," said the little fish.

She turned round and rubbed her eyes. She could not believe what she saw.

Where the vinegar bottle had been was a pretty white cottage with a brass knocker on the front door and red roses climbing the walls.

The old woman opened the gate onto a small garden filled with flowers. "It can't be mine, it can't," she whispered, but there was Malt coming down the path to meet her.

Malt did not know if he was on his head or his paws.

The old woman opened the door into a proper sitting room, with her rocking chair on one side of the fire and Malt's cushion on the other.

Upstairs was a bathroom with hot water. Her hands shook as she turned on the taps – she had never had a tap before. "Lordy! Lordy!"

Malt sat with his tail round his paws and made noises as if to say, "Where is my vinegar bottle?"

But as she went through the rooms again her things, which had suited the vinegar bottle, now looked battered and old.

"It looks terrible bare," said the old woman.

She hestitated, but in a few moments she was calling, "Little fish, little fish."

The water went *bubble bubble bubble* and up he came.

"The cottage is so pretty, I don't know how to thank you, but…"

The little fish was just disappearing when he heard the 'but' and stopped.

"…but I meant a cottage with new furniture. Please, dear little fish…"

"Go home and you will find some," said the little fish.

There was a blue sofa and two blue chairs. A basket was ready for Malt and a new kettle sat on the hob. "Was there ever such a lucky old woman as I?" said the old woman.

Upstairs was a four-poster bed. Inside a new wardrobe hung her 'other' dress – she only had two – and a long mirror. For the first time in her life, the old woman saw herself from head to toe.

"Lordy," she said, "is that really me?" She stared at herself. Her clothes seemed terribly shabby.

"You're a proper old ragbag," she said slowly.

Then she got up and went down to the loch. "Little fish, little fish."

The water went *bubble bubble bubble* and up came the little fish.

Almost before the fish had his head out of the water, the old woman burst out, "I can't live in that lovely cottage dressed like this. I must have some new clothes."

The little fish said, "Look."

At first the old woman did not know where to look. She looked behind her, on each side and up at the sky. Then she looked down and said, "Lordy!" She was wearing a new dress and apron. On her feet were buckled shoes and she had warm white stockings. When she got back to the cottage, she found more beautiful new clothes.

Malt sniffed her and his whiskers went stiff. "You don't smell like my old woman," he seemed to say.

How careful the old woman was when she ate her dinner that day. Not a drop must be spilled on her new dress, and she scolded Malt when his whiskers dribbled milk on the floor.

"Drat that cat! I might dirty my new apron wiping that up." That brought a thought: "How can I possibly clean in my new clothes?"

The next moment she was hurrying down to the loch.

"Little fish, little fish." The old woman sounded out of temper and the fish's fins rose in surprise.

"You can't expect me to do housework in these fine clothes. You said I should have everything I want. Well, I want a maid."

"Go home and you will find one," said the little fish in a quiet, tired voice.

The maid's name was Amelia; she was waiting at the cottage door when the old woman returned.

"Would you like a cup of tea, Ma'am?" she asked. No one had called the old woman 'Ma'am' before.

After her tea the old woman could not settle in her new chair: for one thing it would not rock, and for another Amelia came in and out with her duster. "We're used to being alone, Malt and me," she thought.

The old woman decided to change her clothes. "Well, I have nothing else to do."

She had put on a grey silk dress when she heard the sound of bells. "If it isn't Sunday!" She decided to go to church and show off her new clothes. "Take care of Malt. I shall soon be back, Amelia."

"Yes, Ma'am." Then Amelia said, "You're never going to walk there in those shoes?"

The old woman *had* been going to walk, but the buckled shoes were thin compared to her old clogs.

"No, indeed," she said and she marched down to the loch.

"Little fish. Little fish."

The water went *bubble bubble bubble* and up came the little fish.

"With these new clothes it's a waste to stay at home, so I am going to church." The old woman did not know it but she spoke in a hoity-toity voice.

The fish said nothing but looked at the old woman a little sadly.

"Kindly order me a conveyance" – she did not know how she found such a grand word – "a conveyance, my good fish."

"Go home and you will find one," said the patient little fish.

A cart and pony stood at the cottage gate. Amelia was stroking the pony's mane and giving it lumps of sugar. "Oh Ma'am, isn't it the prettiest little pony in the whole wide world?"

The old woman did not seem to think so; she sniffed in disdain and turned straight back to the loch.

"Little fish. Little fish."

The water went *bubble bubble bubble* and up came the little fish.

"You didn't understand." The old woman sounded almost as if she were scolding. "When I said a conveyance, of course I meant a car. Who goes about in a pony and cart these days?"

"Go home and you will find one," said the little fish, and he went back into the water with a sharp flop.

The pony and trap had gone. In their place was a small red car.

"That stupid fish!" cried the old woman. "I didn't mean a car like that!" And again she turned straight back to the loch.

"Little fish. Little fish." She stamped her foot. The water went *bubble bubble bubble* and up came the little fish.

"What can I do with a niminy car like that?" said the furious old woman. "You know quite well that I can't drive. I meant, of course, a car with a chauffeur like the Queen's. At once, if you please, or I'll be late."

The little fish did not say, "Go home and you will find one," but stood up out of the water on his silver tail.

"You used to curtsey to me," he said. "Yesterday you came and said 'thank you' before you touched a morsel of the dinner I sent you. That was yesterday, only yesterday, but now! You are a greedy, ungrateful old woman. Go back to your vinegar bottle."

Suddenly, the grey silk dress was gone, and the old woman was back in her shabby old dress, her faded print apron and slippers. The cottage, the furniture, the clothes, Amelia and the car had vanished and the vinegar bottle was back in its old place.

Malt ran purring towards his old home.

It was a miserable old woman who crept down to the loch that evening. She stood on the shore and called, "Little fish. Little fish!"

She did not think he would come but the water went *bubble bubble bubble* and up came the little fish.

"What do you want?"

"To say I'm sorry." The old woman wiped her eyes on the corner of her apron. "Forgive me for troubling you, but I'm sorry to have been so rude and ungrateful. You're quite right, little fish. I'm a greedy old woman. I don't know what got into me and that's the truth. I'm sorry and please forgive me. Goodbye, little fish."

She curtsied and turned to go but the little fish called, "Old woman, I'm glad. I thought this was going to be a sad story and it isn't at all. You are still the generous, kind old woman I thought you were. And now I shall make everything come back."

But the old woman shook her head. "Thank you kindly, little fish, but no. Malt and me, we're best in our vinegar bottle. We'll stay as we are, except…"

"Except?" asked the little fish gently.

"If it wouldn't be greedy, do you think, now and then sir, sire, prince, Highness, you could send us a good hot dinner? Why, one of those dinners would keep Malt and me for a week. I'll wash it up," said the old woman.

The old woman still lives in the vinegar bottle.

   As she sits rocking, she often thinks of the little fish who talked.
She knows he was not a dream because every Sunday, as the village
church clock strikes noon, a hot dinner appears on her table,
another by the cushion for Malt.